A Note to Parents

Read to your child...

★ Reading aloud is one of the best ways to develop your child's love of reading. Read together at least 20 minutes each day.

★ Laughter is contagious! Read with feeling. Show your child that reading is fun.

★ Take time to answer questions your child may have about the story. Linger over pages that interest your child.

...and your child will read to you.

★ Follow cues from your child to know when he wants to join in the reading.

★ Support your young reader. Give him a word whenever he asks for it.

★ Praise your child as he progresses. Your encouraging words will build his confidence.

You can help your Level 1 reader.

★ Reading begins with knowing how a book works. Show your child the title and where the story begins.

★ Ask your child to find picture clues on each page. Talk about what is happening in the story.

★ Point to the words as you read so your child can make the connection between the print and the story.

★ Ask your child to point to words she knows.

★ Let your child supply the rhyming words.

Most of all, enjoy your reading time together!

—Bernice Cullinan, Ph.D.,
Professor of Reading, New York University

Reader's Digest Children's Books
Reader's Digest Road, Pleasantville, NY 10570-7000
Copyright © 1999 Reader's Digest Children's Publishing, Inc.
All rights reserved. Reader's Digest Children's Books and All-Star Readers are
trademarks and Reader's Digest is a registered trademark
of The Reader's Digest Association, Inc.
Fisher-Price trademarks are used under license from
Fisher-Price, Inc., a subsidiary of Mattel, Inc., East Aurora, NY 14052.
Printed in Hong Kong.
10 9 8 7 6 5 4 3 2 1

Library of Congress Cataloging-in-Publication Data

Hall, Kirsten.
    We are all different / by Kirsten Hall ; illustrated by Bari Weissman and Linda Hunter.
       p. cm. — (All-star readers. Level 1)
    Summary: Although children are different in appearance, they all have ten toes,
favorite clothes, and love to play.
    ISBN 1-57584-321-8
    [1. Individuality—Fiction. 2. Stories in rhyme.]
    I. Weissman, Bari, ill. II. Hunter, Linda, ill. III Title IV. Series.
PZ7.H1457We   1999   [E]—dc21   99-19547

We Are All Different

by Kirsten Hall
illustrated by Bari Weissman and Linda Hunter

All-Star Readers™

Reader's Digest Children's Books™
Pleasantville, New York • Montréal, Québec

I have different
eyes than you.

Yours are brown
and mine are blue.

I have different hair than you.

Yours is short, and Jane's is, too!

Different ears . . .
a different nose . . .

different fingers . . . different toes.

You wear braces.
So does Dee!

My new glasses help me see.

We have different-colored skin.

Sam has freckles
on his chin.

We may look different, that is true.

But I am also just like you!

We both have eyes.
We have a nose.

We have two ears.
We have ten toes.

We all have mouths.

We all have hair.

We all have clothes
we like to wear.

We all have words we like to say.

We like to run
and jump and play.

Come join the fun,
come play a game.

29

See? While we're different,

we're the same!

Color in the star next to each word you can read.

☆ a	☆ ears	☆ like	☆ so
☆ all	☆ eyes	☆ look	☆ ten
☆ also	☆ fingers	☆ may	☆ than
☆ am	☆ freckles	☆ me	☆ that
☆ and	☆ fun	☆ mine	☆ the
☆ are	☆ game	☆ mouths	☆ to
☆ blue	☆ glasses	☆ my	☆ toes
☆ both	☆ hair	☆ new	☆ too
☆ braces	☆ has	☆ nose	☆ true
☆ brown	☆ have	☆ on	☆ two
☆ but	☆ help	☆ play	☆ we
☆ chin	☆ his	☆ run	☆ wear
☆ clothes	☆ I	☆ Sam	☆ we're
☆ colored	☆ is	☆ same	☆ while
☆ come	☆ Jane's	☆ say	☆ words
☆ Dee	☆ join	☆ see	☆ you
☆ different	☆ jump	☆ short	☆ yours
☆ does	☆ just	☆ skin	